YODA'S GALAXY ATLAS

Written by
Simon Hugo

CONTENTS

DANGER
POINT OF NO
RETURN

INTRODUCTION TO THE GALAXY

A big place the galaxy is! Need the best guide, you will, if a galactic traveler you wish to be … Luckily for you, the best guide to the galaxy I am! Many worlds I have seen, and many times. Every now and again, a vacation I need! Use this book to plan your own breaks, as if sat beside you I am. Even if stuck on Jakku you are—with no starship and no suitcase—adventure far you still can with words alone. A powerful thing the mind of a reader is!

Travel safe and may the Force be with you,

Yoda

DEPARTURES

9

Coruscant Security Forces Ride Along tour

Book a tour—or don't! One way or another, you're coming with us!

Coruscant Open-Top ShuttleBus

Monument Plaza

What Was Alderaan Like?

Come to the talk at 2:30pm on the observation deck

CORELLIA

CHAPTER ONE
CORE WORLDS

Named for their closeness to the Galactic Core,
these worlds boast some of the busiest, wealthiest,
and most technologically advanced civilizations in
the galaxy. If you're looking for a fast-paced city
vacation, there's no better place to go!

CORUSCANT

Nowhere in the galaxy is quite as busy as the galactic capital city-planet. You could spend a lifetime here and never see all of it—even if you live as long as Master Yoda. The sky is always full of ships, and the urban sprawl stretches all around the globe!

Dex's Diner

The best eats in the Coco Town Streets

Enjoy a free ice-cold green fizzle drink

Typical weather

Often cloudy, always computer-controlled.

Where to eat

Dex's Diner
Friendly owner Dexter Jettster needs all four of his arms to keep up with orders at this popular eatery. Find it in the industrial Coco Town district, and be sure to try the special, a club sandwich on therm-zapped (or toasted) bread.

Coruscant Police gunship

Who's who on Coruscant

The Jedi Council
Senior Jedi Masters such as Ki-Adi-Mundi once spent much of their time in the Jedi Temple.

The Senate Guard
The blue uniforms of the Senate Guard are a symbol of Coruscant and its galactic government.

TOP 3 MUST SEES!

1. The Galactic Senate

Politics is never boring in the Senate Chamber, where senators from more than 1,000 worlds gather in flying pods!

2. The Jedi Temple

The Jedi lived and trained here for centuries, until the Emperor turned it into his personal palace.

3. The Underworld

Coruscant's lower levels are dark and scary, but you need to see them to get the planet's full story.

Let's see some ID, shorty!

My identification, you don't need to see!

VOTE PALPATINE FOR EMPEROR

★ ★ ★ ★ ★ ★ ★ ★ ★

HE'S THE ONLY* CHOICE!

*No, really.

SAVE CORUSCANT'S HISTORIC BUILDINGS

DON'T LET THE STONE MITES BITE!

💼 What to pack

1. Your best clothes for a trip to the famous Galaxies Opera House.

2. Your worst clothes so you don't stand out in the Underworld.

3. Breathing gear is also essential in the polluted Underworld.

Shock Troopers
The city police are far from friendly. Don't try asking them for directions!

Droids
There are droids to do everything on Coruscant. Medical droids even carry out life-saving operations!

13

CORELLIA

Corellians are well-known galactic wanderers. It's easy to see why when you visit their homeworld! By day, Corellia's grimy cities are dominated by factories and the pollution they pump out. By night, criminal gangs such as the White Worms rule the streets.

PARENTS— PROTECT YOUR KIDS FROM WORMS

SIGN THEM UP FOR THE IMPERIAL NAVY

Hmm! Stop for the little green guy, all speeders should!

White Worms' landspeeder

Who's who on Corellia

Han Solo
Han was born on Corellia. He lived as a scrumrat, until he escaped the planet to train as a pilot.

Qi'ra
This savvy scrumrat worked for the White Worms alongside Han.

Typical weather

Rain and industrial smog.

DOS AND DON'TS ON CORELLIA

Do watch out for scrumrats—young pickpockets who work for a crime gang.

Don't start talking to any Imperial recruitment officers. You might end up as a mudtrooper!

Do book your return journey well in advance. There can be long lines at the spaceport.

Don't pet the doglike Corellian hounds—their bite is even worse than their bark!

Imperial Patrol speeder

FORTHCOMING EVENTS IN CORONET CITY

This week: **Save the Corellian hounds** fundraiser

Next week: **Save us from the Corellian hounds!** fundraiser

Fresh fish

Visit the Coronet fish markets

Getting around

Renting a landspeeder is the best way to see more of Corellia. But be aware that the fast and flashy M-68 model is a popular target for scrumrat thieves.

Moloch
This member of the White Worms crime gang really is a giant worm!

Rebolt
Thuggish Rebolt was one of the White Worms' favored goons.

15

ALDERAAN

Known throughout the galaxy for its beauty, this peaceful world was once at the top of every traveler's to-do list. But set your coordinates for Alderaan today and all you'll find is the space where it used to be, before it was blown up by the Empire!

WELCOME TO THE ALDERAAN SYSTEM
Please fly carefully through our asteroid field

⭐⭐⭐ Alderaan reviews

DarkLord66
My favorite thing about Alderaan was when it exploded. I can't give it five stars because of all those times when it wasn't exploding.

☆☆☆☆☆

Tantive IV

Who's who in the Alderaan system

Leia Organa
Leia grew up as a princess on Alderaan. She left to lead the fight against the Empire and, later, the First Order.

Bail Organa
Bail and his wife Breha, the Queen of Alderaan, adopted Leia when she was a baby, and raised her to rebel.

Typical weather

Alderaan was known for its fine weather, and snow at high altitudes.

DOS AND DON'TS
IN THE ALDERAAN SYSTEM

Do pay your respects at the asteroid field where Alderaan used to be.

Don't crash your ship into any of the asteroids!

Do locate the nearby star that gave Alderaan its beautiful sunsets.

Don't forget to look out for surviving Alderaanian ships, such as the *Tantive IV*.

What to pack

1. A space suit—if you're planning to get out of your ship.

2. Food and drink—you won't find anywhere to eat here.

3. Tissues—thinking about the end of Alderaan might make you cry!

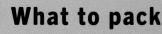

ALDERAAN
We wish you were here!

Raymus Antilles
The captain of the *Tantive IV* was a trusted ally to the Organas.

Cara Dune
Cara's home planet is peace-loving Alderaan.

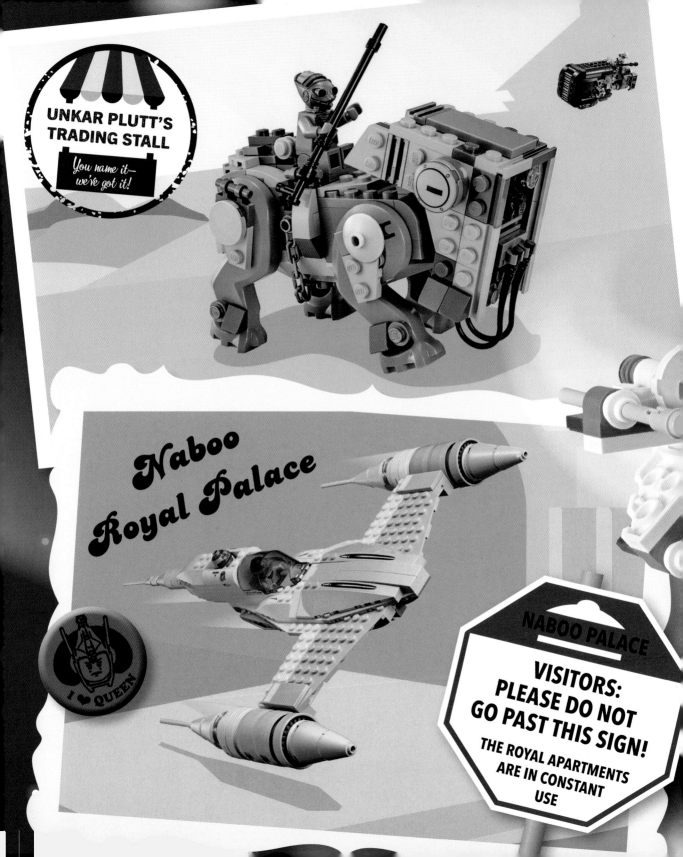

UNKAR PLUTT'S TRADING STALL

You name it— we've got it!

Naboo
Royal Palace

I ♥ QUEEN

NABOO PALACE

VISITORS:
PLEASE DO NOT
GO PAST THIS SIGN!

THE ROYAL APARTMENTS
ARE IN CONSTANT
USE

CHAPTER TWO

INNER AND MID RIM WORLDS

Surrounding the area known as the Core, the Inner and Mid Rims are home to many different species, including the Gungans and the Wookiees. These planets all make good bases from which to explore the wider galaxy.

JAKKU

There's a reason tourists don't go to Jakku, and that reason is sand. If you want sand, there are much nicer places to find it. If you don't want sand, then Jakku has very little to offer you—except for scavengers, out to swipe anything you leave lying around!

LOOK OUT!

THERE'S A LUGGABEAST ABOUT!

Teedo zatana tappan-aboo!

What to pack

1. Plenty of snacks—food is hard to come by here!

2. Trashed tech for trading at Niima Outpost.

3. Goggles and boots to keep the sand out of your eyes and socks!

Teedo riding a luggabeast

Who's who on Jakku

Rey
Rey was left on Jakku as a child and grew up here all alone.

Finn
Finn came to Jakku as a stormtrooper, but left it as a free man!

Typical weather

Scorching in the day, but freezing at night.

FIRST ORDER

SAND

EVEN MORE SAND

MORE SAND

Getting around

You'll need your own transport to get around on Jakku. Why not build a speeder from spare parts, just like Rey did?

Talk Teedospeak I do not!

TOP 3 MUST SEES!

1. Starship Graveyard

Go scavenging for souvenirs among the ships that crashed in the desert during the final battle between the Empire and the Rebellion.

2. Niima Outpost

Jakku's spaceport is the first thing you'll see on the planet. You'll want to come back here—so that you can leave!

3. Goazon Badlands

Before she became a galactic hero, Rey lived in a rusting Imperial walker that lay on its side in this part of the desert.

Lor San Tekka
This wise old man kept a secret for Luke Skywalker on Jakku.

Teedo
These scavengers travel on luggabeasts, looking for loot in the desert.

NAVIGATING NIIMA

Not much happens on Jakku, but anything that does happens at Niima Outpost, the planet's only spaceport. The name to know around here is Unkar Plutt—a mean trader who sells spaceships and spare parts. He can get you anything you need, but his thugs might steal it back again!

Traveler's tip

Be on the look out for bargains at Niima Outpost. For several years, Unkar Plutt had the *Millennium Falcon* up for sale here—until Rey and Finn "borrowed" it!

VEHICLES LEFT AT OWN RISK.
UNATTENDED QUADJUMPERS MAY BE DESTROYED.

Unkar's trading stall

Snap a selfie at Niima Gate!

DOS AND DON'TS AT NIIMA OUTPOST

Do trade junk for food at Unkar's stall.

Don't expect to get a good meal.

Do watch your back at all times.

Don't watch Unkar's back. Or his front. They're both horrible!

BEWARE
UNKAR PLUTT'S THUGS PATROL THIS AREA

Keep safe!

Up with Plutt's plots I will not put!

Niima for droids

Mechanical travelers should take extra care on Jakku. Never take your eyes off your owner, and never let anyone take your eyes off you!

23

TAKODANA

You can really get away from it all on Takodana—that's why smugglers and scoundrels like to hide out here! The forests and lakes are a must for nature-lovers, but the biggest draw is the lively castle of pirate queen Maz Kanata.

Typical weather

Sunny and humid.

Traveler's tip

Maz's castle used to be a Jedi temple. Ask her nicely and she might show you some of its ancient treasures!

The Skywalker lightsaber

Don't miss
THE GIANT STATUE OF MAZ!
Takodana Tours

Who's who on Takodana

Maz Kanata
Maz has been welcoming guests to her castle for at least a thousand years!

Han Solo
Maz is always happy to see this rebel hero swagger into her castle.

We didn't miss THE GIANT STATUE OF MAZ!

DOS AND DON'TS
AT MAZ'S CASTLE

Do whatever Maz tells you to do!

Don't start any fights. That's always good advice, but here it's a rule.

Do ask Maz about her centuries of travel and adventure.

Don't stay longer than one night—it gets expensive!

I thought you'd be taller!

A lot, I get that.

Maz's castle

💼 What to pack

1. A musical instrument—if you play well, you can stay at the castle for free!

2. A swimsuit for a dip in Nymeve Lake.

3. Credits—nearly every guest at the castle has something to sell!

General Leia
Leia and Han were reunited on Takodana after years apart.

Chewbacca
Maz likes to call Chewie her "boyfriend." He doesn't seem to mind!

NABOO

A trip to the lush and watery world of Naboo is like two vacations in one! Start in the royal city of Theed, where humans spend their days in grand palaces and plazas. Then, dip a toe into the underwater world of the Gungans—but watch out for giant sea beasts!

You can't go wrongo in a tribubble bongo!

Gungan submarine rides daily

For low-flying aircraft you must watch out!

Naboo starfighter

Who's who in Naboo

Padmé Amidala
The most famous Queen of Naboo is far friendlier than her formal face-paints make her look!

Jar Jar Binks
This goofy Gungan helped make peace between his people and Naboo's human inhabitants.

Typical weather

Plenty of sunshine with bursts of heavy rain.

TOP 3 MUST SEES!

1. Theed Royal Palace

Wise rulers like Queen Amidala address their people (and have people to dress them) in this beautiful clifftop castle.

2. Otoh Gunga

Every Gungan in this underwater city stays warm and dry, thanks to its big, bubble-shaped force fields.

3. Festival of Light

This colorful celebration of Naboo has been held once a year for more than 800 years!

GIANT SEA MONSTERS!

What to pack

1. Fish food—to make sure *you* don't become fish food!

2. Bring your best clothes for a walk through fashionable Theed.

3. Bring your best boots for a hike through the humid swamps!

Getting around

When battle droids attacked this world, they used Armored Assault Tanks. You'll get a warmer welcome in a Flash Speeder!

Roos Tarpals
Like all Gungans, Roos is an amphibian, so is happy living on land or underwater.

Sheev Palpatine
Believe it or not, the evil Emperor was born on Naboo!

KASHYYYK

The home of the Wookiees is a woodland paradise, but even paradise has its problems! Over the years, Kashyyyk has suffered from a droid invasion and a long period of Imperial rule. It's best to find a Wookiee companion for your travels here.

DROID GUNSHIPS START FOREST FIRES!

Report all sightings to your local Wookiee warden

COME TO WULLFFWARRO'S WORLD OF WOOD

For classic Kashyyyk crafts. Bowcasters, battle shields, and more—all made from finely carved wroshyr!

Back again, those pesky droids are!

Who's who on Kashyyyk

Chewbacca
Han Solo's best friend and Rey's copilot knows every part of his planet —if only he did tours!

Tarfful
This brave warrior led the fight against an invading droid army during the Clone Wars.

Typical weather

Warm with rainy seasons.

Phrasebook

Shyriiwook:

Yes—*Mmmmmmrrrrr!*
No—*Rwww!*

Wookiee gunship

TOP 3 MUST SEES!

1. Treetop cities

Wookiee settlements such as the capital city, Kachirho, are built into the sides and tops of giant wroshyr trees.

2. The Origin Tree

Kashyyyk has many huge trees, but few can compete with this one, which rises above the clouds.

3. Woodland wildlife

Be on the lookout for can-cell bugs, which are said to bring good luck, and flame beetles that glow and sometimes explode!

What to pack

1. A hairbrush—it's an honor to be asked to comb a Wookiee.

2. A translator unit—there are more than 150 words for wood!

3. Tweezers—you might need to remove a splinter or two …

BEWARE! ANGRY WOOKIES

Commander Gree
Clone trooper Gree fought alongside Yoda and Tarfful at the Battle of Kashyyyk.

Luminara Unduli
This Jedi Master fell in battle while defending Kashyyyk against the droid army.

PASAANA

Pasaana is a party planet—but only once every 42 years! Be sure to time your visit around the Festival of the Ancestors, when the usually quiet Forbidden Valley erupts in celebration of the past and future. Come here at any other time and all you'll find is dust farms!

Transport speeder

Who's who on Pasaana

Lando Calrissian
Rebel hero Lando went to Pasaana to track down Ochi. He wanted to find the Sith relic hunter to stop the First Order's dangerous plans.

D-O
This little droid was left all alone on Pasaana for many years, until he made a new droid friend in BB-8.

Knights of Ren
When the villainous Knights of Ren came to Pasaana, they missed the memo about colorful clothes!

WHY TOUR THE GALAXY ...
WHEN YOU COULD BE GATHERING DUST?

Life's speck-tacular when you work on a dust farm—and there are regular holidays, too!*

*Holidays once every 42 years.

Typical weather

Dry with occasional dust storms.

DOS AND DON'TS ON PASAANA

Do accept the flower necklaces offered by the planet's Aki-Aki people.

Don't eat too much of their famous candy!

Do join in with the joyful crowd dances.

Don't dance your way into the quicksand fields!

Around here somewhere, that festival is!

Festival of the Ancestors

Forbidden Valley, Pasaana

Celebrating peace, love, and flower power!

FEATURING THE "LIDO HEY" DANCERS • KITE DISPLAYS • TRIBUTE BANDS (MAXIMUM REBO, FIGRIN F'AN, THE BOOTLEG SNOOTLES) • AND LOTS AND LOTS OF CANDY!!!

All acts TBC

Flower garlands for sale

Getting around

Low-flying skimmers and treaded vehicles are the best way to keep from sinking in the sand on Pasaana. The First Order used treadspeeder bikes when they came here.

JEDHA

For many years, Jedha was the place to go to find out about the Force and the history of the Jedi. But when the first Death Star destroyed Jedha City, this special place was lost forever. Now there is nothing left to see, but the Force is still strong here!

Jedha City
★ ★ ★
Passed the Death Star's first superlaser test

DOS AND DON'TS ON JEDHA

Ruined this place the Empire did!

Do look for kyber crystals, which are used to make lightsabers.

Do try to feel the Force energies that made this place special to the Jedi.

Don't look for the great Kyber Temple—it isn't there anymore.

Don't try too hard—not everyone can sense it!

Who's who on Jedha

Bodhi Rook
Jedha-born Bodhi was an Imperial pilot before he joined the Rebellion.

Baze Malbus
Baze is one of the Guardians of the Whills, pledged to defend the Kyber Temple against attackers.

★★★ **Jedha City**
reviews

LookWhosTarkin
Great for target practice. Things have really blown up since I first came here.

☆☆☆☆☆

CaptainCassian
Such a shame this place is gone now. My droid, K-2SO, really loved it.

☆☆☆☆☆

K-2SO
Cassian made me come here. I hated every second of it.

☆☆☆☆☆

Hologram of Imperial Assault Hovertank on Jedha

Visit the haunted
Catacombs of Cadera

[**CLOSED**]

Just half a day's walk from Jedha City!

"Definitely not a rebel base"

TOUR THE IMPERIAL KYBER MINES

[**OUT OF BUSINESS**]

FREE ENTRY*
*You may be required to mine up to 10 crystals for the Empire before you are allowed to leave.

Typical weather

Permanent winter, but no snow.

 **Chirrut Îmwe**
Baze's best friend is a fellow Guardian, who relies on the Force to guide him through life as a warrior monk.

 **Jyn Erso**
This rebel hero came to Jedha to find the secrets of the Death Star.

VANDOR

Winter sports fans will love Vandor's snow-covered slopes and hiking trails, but hardly anyone chooses to make a home here. Away from the few small settlements, the only signs of life you'll see are farmers tending to shaggy kod'yok cattle, and the occasional high-speed cargo train snaking between the peaks.

 ## What to pack

1. Winter wear—even stormtroopers wear fur coats here.

2. Goggles to keep the stinging cold out of your eyes.

3. Mountaineering gear—or a jet pack!

Get off our train!

Hrmph!

Imperial cargo train

Who's who on Vandor

Lando Calrissian
Lando was playing cards at the Lodge saloon when he first met Han Solo. He didn't think much of the scruffy pilot.

Tobias Beckett
Career criminal Beckett came to Vandor to hijack an Imperial cargo train.

DOS AND DON'TS ON VANDOR

Mount Redolava
Elevation:
2,990 meters
(9,810 feet)

Do visit the Lodge saloon in Fort Ypso village.

Do enjoy a kod'yok ride across the snow-capped mountains.

Don't go to the droid-fighting arena. Support droid rights!

Don't try to hitch a ride on an Imperial cargo train!

FOLLOW THE HERD!

EAT, DRINK, AND STAY AT THE LODGE ON VANDOR

1 free cup of hot kod'yok milk with this coupon.

Getting around

Sadly, the train network built by the Empire is not for public use. However, Cloud-Rider pirates have proved that you can match the railroad's speed and route by flying repulsorlift swoop bikes.

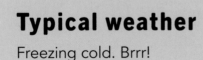

Typical weather

Freezing cold. Brrr!

Enfys Nest
Nest and her Cloud-Rider pirates came to Vandor to hijack Beckett's hijack!

Rio Durant
This four-armed Ardennian pilot was part of Beckett's gang.

35

CLOUD CITY

Cloud Car Rental

Call
5263122

The Forest Moon of Endor

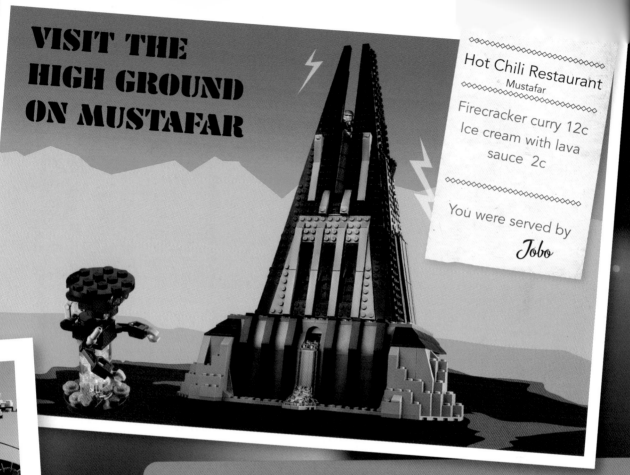

VISIT THE HIGH GROUND ON MUSTAFAR

CHAPTER THREE
OUTER RIM WORLDS

Planets are few and far between on the vast outer edge of the galaxy. Some are home to isolated cultures, while others have just one or two dwellers—or can't even be lived on! Come here when you want to get away from it all.

CLOUD CITY

This fabulous flying city was built for gas mining, but its upper levels are now filled with lively stores, restaurants, and hotels. They aren't cheap, so don't come here unless you have credits to spare. But concentrate on saving now, and you could have your head in the clouds in no time at all!

TOP 3 MUST SEES!

1. Bespin sunsets

Cloud City hangs in the sky above the gas planet Bespin. Don't miss the best views of Bespin as its sun goes down.

2. Luxurious hotels

Kick back at one of the magnificent hotels. You may even spot some rich and famous faces from across the galaxy!

3. Administrator's Palace

Located at the very top of Cloud City, this lavish home once belonged to the rebel hero Lando Calrissian!

Cloud City

The gale force is strong up here!

Life's a gas on Cloud City!

Who's who in Cloud City

Lando Calrissian
Lando was a Baron of Cloud City before he joined the Rebel Alliance. He was in charge of all that went on there—legal or otherwise!

Lobot
This Bespin native has computer implants. These allow him to keep Cloud City's systems running with his thoughts alone.

Boba Fett
Bounty hunter Boba left Cloud City with a unique souvenir— Han Solo frozen in a block of carbonite!

Getting around

No trip to Bespin is complete without renting a twin-pod cloud car. Use it to shuttle between the different levels of the planet's atmosphere.

Red Cloud Car Company
Helmets must be worn

A LONGER STAY IN CLOUD CITY

Most travelers choose to visit Cloud City for the glamour of its upper levels, but some like to see its industrial lower levels, too. Hardworking Ugnaughts mine Tibanna gas here. They prepare it for sale in carbon-freezing chambers, which are well worth a tour.

And here is where I push the button.

DOS AND DON'TS
ON THE LOWER LEVELS

Do use the handrails—there are some big drops!

Don't get distracted—you could easily lose a hand here.

Do ask the Ugnaughts about the carbon freezing process.

Don't volunteer to take part in a demonstration!

UGNAUGHTS!

Make your fortune out of THIN AIR as a

CLOUD CITY MINER!

Carbon-freezing chamber

Lando Calrissian says:

Put BESPIN TIBANNA GAS in YOUR hyperdrive

And fly like a Falcon!

Hmm. For the Han Solo mold, how much?

⭐⭐⭐ Carbon-freezing chamber reviews

DarkLord66
I had Han Solo frozen in carbonite here, and found all the staff to be friendly and helpful. They didn't even mind when my son caused a scene in the chamber!

☆☆☆☆☆

HanTheMan
If you have to be frozen in carbonite, I can't think of a better place to do it than Cloud City. They let me pull a funny face and everything!

☆☆☆☆☆

PigsMightFly
Thanks for the positive comments! Your feedback is important to us Ugnaughts, and helps us provide service with a smile.

💼 What to pack

1. A landing permit to park your ship in the city.

2. A fashionable cape to wear on the upper levels.

3. An Ugnaught phrasebook to get by on the lower levels.

Why not have your **FAMILY REUNION** at CLOUD CITY?

HOTH

When the Empire came to freezing Hoth, they didn't just bring snowshoes—they brought huge walkers called AT-ATs! Travel here today for the winter sports, and you'll have to ski between the walkers they left behind. These metal monsters may look scary, but they actually make a good obstacle course!

TRAVEL BY TAUNTAUN

The warmer way to get around!

🧳 What to pack

1. Your biggest, warmest coat.

2. Skis, a snowboard, or a sled.

3. A portable heater—or lots of extra-thick socks!

AT-AT walker

Who's who on Hoth

General Veers
This Imperial officer led the AT-AT assault on the rebels when they went into hiding on Hoth.

AT-AT drivers
These soldiers command the gigantic AT-AT (All Terrain Armored Transport) walkers.

DOS AND DON'TS ON HOTH

Do take a ride on one of the friendly, furry tauntauns.

Don't stay out at night—you'll literally be frozen stiff!

Do make the most of the snow during the day.

Don't wander into the path of a wampa. They are also furry, but they are very unfriendly!

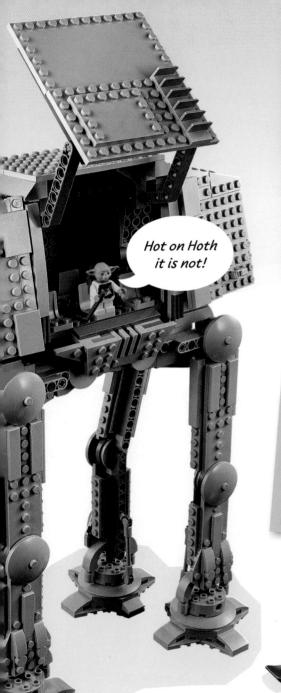

Hot on Hoth it is not!

It's cool!

HANG OUT AND CHILL IN THE ICE CAVES OF HOTH!

Beeeeeeeeep!

WATCH OUT FOR WAMPAS!

Imperial snowtroopers
These cold-climate specialists have central heating built into their body armor!

Probe droids
The Empire sent lots of these droids to Hoth on a mission to find a rebel base.

EXPLORING ECHO BASE

The only sign of civilization on Hoth is a rebel base in the ice. The massive structure has impressive defenses, huge starship hangars, and an advanced medical center. But the rebels only got to use it for a few weeks, before the Empire arrived and turned up the heat!

WARNING! ICY FLOORS!

(OH, AND WAMPAS)

Hello!

TOP 3 MUST SEES!

1. Lookout towers

Climb the sentry points around Echo Base to view the frozen scene where the Battle of Hoth took place.

2. Blast doors

Echo Base's impressive double doors were designed to keep the heat in and the Empire out!

3. Medical center

This is where Luke Skywalker recovered in a healing bacta tank after he was captured by a wampa.

So that is why "Echo Base" they call it!

Hello!

★★★ Echo Base reviews

HanTheMan
Sure it's cold, but get a big hood like mine and you'll feel as warm as a Wookiee!

☆☆☆☆☆

Toryn_Farr
I was a technician at Echo Base. To read my review of it, visit my blog, "Farr Far Away"!

☆☆☆☆☆

🤖 **Hoth** for droids

Be careful not to let your joints freeze on this ice planet. Make time for a soothing oil bath if you can.

Getting around

If you can't get the hang of tauntaun riding (or you just don't like the smell), why not travel by snowspeeder? The rebels were forced to leave these cool craft behind when they abandoned Echo Base.

ENDOR

When travelers talk about Endor, they usually mean the Forest Moon of Endor rather than the planet of the same name. Make sure you head for the Forest Moon if you're hoping to see some Ewoks. Treat these cuddly-looking creatures with respect and they will do the same to you!

Phrasebook

Ewokese:

*Hello—**Yaa-yaah!***
*Hooray—**Yub nub!***

Getting around

Speeder bikes are the quickest way to get around the forest. Just make sure that you are able to dodge the massive tree trunks!

Bright Tree Village

Typical weather

Mild by day, cold at night.

Who's who on Endor

Wicket W. Warrick
This young Ewok knows the woods like the back of his paw. If you can find him, he's the ideal guide to Endor!

Chief Chirpa
Consider it an honor if you get to meet the wise old chief of Bright Tree Village.

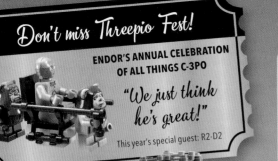

Traveler's tip

Don't leave this system without dipping a toe into Kef Bir—the Ocean Moon of Endor! A friendly tribe of former stormtroopers lives here, led by the freedom fighter Jannah.

LET YOUR HAIR DOWN IN BRIGHT TREE VILLAGE

As visited by the famous Princess Leia!

Quicker than climbing, getting caught is!

DOS AND DON'TS
ON ENDOR

Do look up—the Ewoks live in treetop villages.

Don't forget to look down— Ewoks also lay traps on the ground!

Do let the Ewoks escort you to their village homes.

Don't let them eat you when you get there!

Tour the forest from above!
MOON GLIDER TOURS

⚠ **Watch out for Ewok traps!**

Logray
Ask nicely, and this magical Ewok shaman may perform a ritual to bring you good luck!

47

CRAIT

Crait is so unloved that it doesn't even feature on the latest star charts. This makes it perfect for getting off the familiar tourist track! To find it, you'll need to ask directions from an old rebel who remembers hiding in the abandoned mines here, or an even older miner!

Resistance ski speeder

Getting around

The trailing fin of a ski speeder is great for stirring up the salt to reveal the red crystals below. But so are the giant footprints of a First Order AT-M6 walker!

PLEASE DO NOT PET THE VULPTICES!

By order of the Nupayuni Mining Consortium, Crait Division

Typical weather

Sunny, with occasional crystalstorms.

Who's who on Crait

Caluan Ematt
When Kylo Ren cornered the Resistance here, this old rebel led the fight against the First Order.

Poe Dameron
The Battle of Crait began when Poe launched a daring ski speeder raid on the First Order's invading forces.

★★★ Crait review

snowtrooper4life
I came here expecting snow! Whoever heard of a salt trooper?!

☆☆☆☆☆

TOP 3 MUST SEES!

1. Crait's true colors

Kick away its ghostly white salt crust and Crait is exposed as a vivid red crystal world!

2. Glass animals

Sparkling crystal-covered fur makes the foxlike vulptex one of Crait's most unusual creatures.

3. Secret base

An abandoned crystal mine forms the basis of an old rebel hideout that was also used by the Resistance.

Beware! abandoned mines!

LOST?
Follow the vulptices' path!

You said this planet was great!

Crait, I said it was!

Rose Tico
Resistance engineer Rose saved Finn's life during the Battle of Crait.

TATOOINE

Looking to catch some sun? Then come to Tatooine—it has two of them! The planet is mostly desert, which might sound a little dry, but some of the most important events in the galaxy have revolved around this place. That makes it a key destination on cosmic history tours!

Phrasebook

Jawaese:

*Let's go—**Utinni**
Hands off!—**Togo Togu!***

CAUTION—PODRACERS CROSSING!

I've been stuck in this desert for 35 years!

Well, slow dewback, you chose to ride!

DESERT RACE IT'S ACE!

★ ★ ★

WE NEED SCRAP

Sandtrooper riding a dewback

Who's who on Tatooine

Jawas
Buy a souvenir from these tiny traders, who scavenge the deserts in mighty sandcrawler machines.

Anakin Skywalker
The boy who would become Darth Vader was born on Tatooine, where he built C-3PO.

TOP 3 MUST SEES!

1. Mos Espa Podracing Arena

Blink and you might miss the fastest race in the galaxy! The crowds are huge, the rules are unclear, and the atmosphere is electric!

2. Jabba's Palace

Book ahead to see this beautiful old monastery, now owned by Tatooine celebrity Jabba the Hutt. He isn't a fan of unexpected guests!

3. The Dune Sea

Cruise the "sea" (it's actually just sand!) in a speedy skiff, or take your time on the back of a big green dewback.

Typical weather

Scorching heat and constant threat of sandstorms.

Getting around

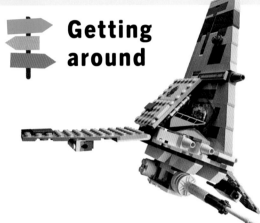

Rent a T-16 skyhopper to see Tatooine from way up in the air. Or go by low-gliding landspeeder to see the planet from very slightly up in the air!

DAILY DROID MARKET
Just follow the huge sandcrawler tracks!

What to pack

1. Goggles and scarves to protect from sandstorms.

2. Water—it is very hard to come by!

3. Spare parts to trade with the local Jawas.

Luke Skywalker
Years after Anakin left the planet, Luke was raised here by his Uncle Owen and Aunt Beru.

Sandtroopers
These specialized stormtroopers combed the desert for rebel droids during the Imperial era.

INTO MOS EISLEY

When you're done with the desert, head next to Tatooine's most famous town. Mos Eisley is a hive of fun, but also plenty of villainy. Simply steer clear of anyone with a blaster in their hand or a bounty on their head, and you will find the Mos Eisley you're looking for!

Cantina Specials
—Beverages—

Blue Milk

Black Melon Milk

Jawa Juice
(Does not contain Jawa)

Tatooine Sunset Tea
(Two for the price of one)

Where to eat

Chalmun's Spaceport Cantina
If you're looking for lively music and even livelier locals, Mos Eisley's main eating and drinking spot is the only place to be. The cantina is named for its Wookiee owner, but the day-to-day boss is Tatooine-born Wuher. Make friends with him and you'll always be welcome here!

Cup of swamp tea, I would like.

Huh?

Chalmun's
Spaceport Cantina

★★★ Cantina reviews

BountyH
The food isn't the best, but the dim lighting is handy for secret meetings.
☆☆☆☆☆

Jawa68
Their no Jawa policy is very annoying!
☆☆☆☆☆

DOS AND DON'TS IN MOS EISLEY

Do keep an eye on your valuables.

Don't assume that all eating establishments will welcome your droids.

Do remember which of the 362 starship docking bays you parked in.

Don't miss Figrin D'an's band at Chalmun's Spaceport Cantina!

Coming soon:

The **Max Rebo** Band

Ask for Spaceport Bay 3-5!

MAROONED IN MOS EISLEY?

Pull in at PELI'S PIT DROIDS for all your starship repair requirements!

No droids

Greed0
I haven't been here yet, but I'm really looking forward to it!
☆☆☆☆☆

A DAY IN THE WASTES

When Obi-Wan Kenobi hid himself and the young Luke Skywalker on Tatooine, few people had heard of the Jundland Wastes. But the Skywalker legend travels at lightspeed, and now everyone knows that this is where Luke grew up! Today it's a must-see for intrepid travelers, such as Rey and BB-8.

Bantha Taxi. Reliable, it is. Nice smelling, it is not.

TOP 3 MUST SEES!

1. Lars Moisture Farm

There are moisture farms all over Tatooine, but this one is where Luke lived before he joined the Rebellion.

2. Obi-Wan's Hut

This simple structure is a long way from the Lars' place. You'll need a landspeeder to see both in one day!

3. Banthas

These big shaggy beasts roam the Jundland Wastes in wild herds and are also ridden by Tusken Raiders.

Traveler's tip

Tusken Raiders are easily startled. Try not to scare them off, as they'll only come back in greater numbers.

Who's who in the Jundland Wastes

Tusken Raiders
Keep away from these scary desert dwellers. They guard their territory with spiky gaffi sticks!

Obi-Wan Kenobi
This Jedi Master went by the name of Ben when he lived here, keeping an eye on Luke from afar.

Owen Lars
The owner of the Lars Moisture Farm raised Luke Skywalker like a son.

Obi-Wan's Hut

NOT WELCOME HERE

Phrasebook

Tusken:

*Hello—**Arrgh!***
*Run!—**Huurrugh!***

55

DUNE SEA SAFARI

Leave your swimwear at home—Tatooine's Dune Sea is actually a vast, dry desert! The Sea surrounds the Jundland Wastes and separates the towns of Mos Espa and Mos Eisley. It is home to many magnificent but *very* dangerous creatures. Make sure you see them all before they see you!

Scuffed skiff?

Revitalize your repulsorcraft with

SKIFF GUARD
FAST-ACTION
SCUFF REMOVER

I'm free!

DOS AND DON'TS
IN THE DUNE SEA

Do seek out the Great Pit of Carkoon. It is home to the huge and multi-tentacled Sarlacc monster.

Don't get too close to the pit. You will get eaten and very slowly digested!

Do look for signs of giant krayt dragons shifting beneath the sands.

Don't stick around if the sand starts to shift beneath your feet!

Sarlacc pit

Getting around

Simple flying platforms called skiffs let you explore the desert in the open air. Rent one from Jabba the Hutt's palace. Just be careful not to fall out of it—or to fall out with Jabba!

Now open

THE GAMORREAN GUARD MEMORIAL GARDEN AND RANCOR MONSTER EXPERIENCE CENTER

Jabba's Palace, Dune Sea, Tatooine

Don't miss feeding times!

Knew you were hard to swallow, I did!

HERE BE DRAGONS!

Sarlacc pit reviews

Jabba_Jabbers
In the belly of my all-powerful Sarlacc, you will find out what it's like to be digested—or your money back!

☆☆☆☆☆

BountyHunter4Hire
I was swallowed by the Sarlacc, and it took me years to get out. Allow extra time for your visit if you plan to get swallowed, too.

☆☆☆☆☆

HanTheMan
I don't know what all the fuss is about. I didn't see anything.

☆☆☆☆☆

Phrasebook

Huttese:

Let's go—**Boska**
Money—**Moulee-rah**

57

GEONOSIS

Don't bring any bug repellent to this desert world—the intelligent insects that live here really won't like it! Geonosis is famous as the planet where the Clone Wars started, and where the Empire's first Death Star was built. For these reasons and more, nobody likes the place very much!

BEWARE! FLASH FLOODS AND METEORS

Dwarf spider droid

Leftovers from the Clone Wars these droids are!

DOS AND DON'TS ON GEONOSIS

Do marvel at the towering hives where the Geonosians live and work.

Don't pour hot water into their hives. They positively hate that.

Do seek out the huge arena where giant alien beasts once battled.

Don't stick around to see if any of the giant beasts still survive!

Who's who in Geonosis

Poggle the Lesser
Archduke Poggle ruled Geonosis during the Clone Wars, setting his people against the Jedi.

Count Dooku
This Sith Lord schemed with Poggle to create a vast droid army in Geonosis' factory hives.

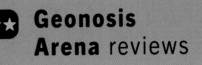

– TONIGHT –
at the Geonosis Arena

ATTACK OF THE ACKLAY—LIVE!*

*First three rows may get eaten

Typical weather

Very dry, with occasional rain and asteroid storms.

Geonosis Arena reviews

Padme_AN
This horrible place promotes cruelty to monsters. Especially the ones I had to beat up in order to escape!

☆☆☆☆☆

Obi-1
Best seats in the house. I could really feel the monsters breathing down my neck!

☆☆☆☆☆

Homing spider droid

Getting around

Geonosians use the wings on their backs to fly short distances. For longer journeys they favor a Flitknot speeder, which can also be used by humans and droids.

WELCOME TO GEONOSIS

Home of Baktoid Combat Automata, makers of the B1 BATTLE DROID

"It's the bugs that make our droids!"

Super Battle Droids
All kinds of droids were built on Geonosis, but these were some of the scariest!

Stass Allie
This Jedi Master was part of a team that came to Geonosis to stop Dooku and Poggle's plans.

MUSTAFAR

The dark side of the Force is strong on Mustafar, so Sith Lords love to take their vacations here. Darth Vader built himself a home on the planet, surrounded by fiery lava fields. Very few people ever come to visit it—and you would do well to stay away as well!

Visit the ancient Sith shrine on Mustafar ...

... and you'll never leave!

Our friendly tour guides say: "Find us under Darth Vader's fortress. Please, someone find us!"

TOP 3 MUST SEES!

1. Vader's fortress

If you must see Mustafar, the main attraction is this terrifying tower. Just don't try to go inside!

2. Lava mines

Valuable minerals can be extracted from the planet's lava, but it's hot and horrible work.

3. Lava fleas

The bugs here are so big that Mustafarians ride on the fleas, rather than the other way around!

MINE TOURS

(Beware the lava!)

Typical weather

Dark and stormy.

Good for getting around, mining robots are!

Who's who
on Mustafar

Darth Vader
When he isn't out conquering the galaxy, the Dark Lord of the Sith likes to relax in his Mustafar fortress.

Anakin Skywalker
Anakin came to Mustafar on a mission for the Emperor, and sealed his fate to become a cyborg Sith Lord.

Nute Gunray
This villainous Neimoidian sided with the Sith, but Darth Vader betrayed him on Mustafar.

Royal Guard
The guards in Vader's fortress match Mustafar's lava-red color scheme.

Don't forget your heat-resistant clothes!

LAVA FLEA RIDES
Hop-on, hop-off parasite-seeing tours.

"We're itching to serve you!"

Darth Vader's fortress

61

AJAN KLOSS

This jungle moon is as green as Yoda himself—and just as lively, with new species being discovered every day. Its existence was kept secret for many years, making it an ideal Resistance base. But when the First Order was finally defeated, everyone was welcome here for the after-party!

Ajan Kloss

Do your Jedi training here!

What to pack

1. Insect repellent—this moon is buggy!

2. Extra clothes—you're sure to sweat in the heat here.

3. A shovel—to dig for evidence of the ancient Kloss civilization.

Like being back on Dagobah, it is!

I spotted a zymod on Ajan Kloss

Who's who on Ajan Kloss

Snap Wexley
This starfighter pilot was one of the first to join the Resistance. He went on to fly missions from D'Qar, Crait, and Ajan Kloss.

Kaydel Connix
Lieutenant Kaydel Connix worked with Rose Tico to set up the Resistance base on Ajan Kloss.

Typical weather

Hot and humid; sometimes stormy.

PARTY IN THE CAVE!

DJ droids • Lightsaber glowsticks • Outdoor jungle area • And more!

Now every week at Klosslands, Ajan Kloss Free entry for Resistance members

PARTY ON THE MOON WHERE THE SUN NEVER SETS!

★★★ Ajan Kloss review

LeiaSOS
I did my Jedi training here. I liked it so much that when I came back I brought the whole Resistance!

☆ ☆ ☆ ☆ ☆

X-wing

TOP 3 MUST SEES!

1. Resistance base

General Leia and the Resistance planned the fall of the First Order from this huge cave in the Klosslands jungle.

2. Color-changing zymods

Keep an eye out for these difficult-to-spot creatures, which live in the broadleaf trees.

3. Midnight sun

It is never entirely dark here, thanks to sunlight reflecting off Ajara (the planet that Ajan Kloss orbits).

R2-D2

When C-3PO's mind was wiped, Artoo was able to restore his memories on Ajan Kloss.

SCARIF

Scarif was an unspoiled beach paradise—until the Empire built a vault there to hide their secrets! They sealed the planet off with a deflector shield and filled it with sand-colored shoretroopers. A rebel strike destroyed the shield, but you'll still see Imperial landing pads on some of the best sunbathing spots ...

> OK, you can play volleyball here! Just put me down!

> Hrm!

DOS AND DON'TS ON SCARIF

Do stretch out on the sand beneath an areca nut palm tree.

Don't accidentally stretch out on a sand-colored shoretrooper!

Do remember the brave rebels who came here to steal the Death Star plans.

Don't expect to see the Citadel vault they stole them from. The Empire blew it up!

> SEE SCARIF from the top of the CITADEL TOWER.
>
> *"It's a blast!"*
>
> CLOSED OWING TO PRIOR DEATH STAR VISIT

Who's who on Scarif

Orson Krennic
Director Krennic took charge of Imperial operations on Scarif when he realized the rebels were heading there.

Jyn Erso
This determined rebel pretended to be an Imperial technician to sneak into the Empire's base on Scarif.

Typical weather

Clear blue sunny skies.

💼 What to pack

1. Shorts and swimwear.

2. Binoculars for bird-watching.

3. Death Star plans for beach reading.

VISIT SCARIF

A tropical paradise

You are now approaching the **SCARIF DEFLECTOR SHIELD**

Please drive carefully through our **SHIELD GATE**
And have your ship's CLEARANCE CODE ready!

Getting around

There are lots of landing pads on Scarif, making it easy to take off and land on the many small islands. The Empire deployed high-speed TIE Strikers here, while the rebels paid a visit in U-wing fighters.

Imperial landing pad

Cassian Andor
Like Jyn, Cassian was part of the rebel crew that came here to discover the secrets of the Death Star.

Shoretroopers
These Imperial soldiers are dressed for the beach, in lightweight sandy armor.

DAGOBAH

Some planets are always swamped with tourists. Others are just swamped with swamps. Dagobah is one of the latter, where it is hard to tell where the land ends and the bogs begin. Only Yoda has ever made a home here, after he learned of its connection to the Force.

Where to eat

Yoda's Hut

If you're hungry, eat here—because it's the only place to eat. Tuck in to Yoda's favorites: Mud and Bug Soup or Swamp Stew. No, they don't sound (or taste) delicious, but they will do.

Welcome to
DAGOBAH
POPULATION: 000,001

TOP 3 MUST SEES!

1. Yoda's Hut

Master Yoda built his home from gnarltree wood, stones, and mud. It may be small and simple, but it's the only place to stay!

2. Cave of Evil

Get close to this cave to feel the chill of the dark side. But don't go inside unless you want to face your worst fears!

3. Dragonsnake Bog

It may not be pretty (and yes, there are dragonsnakes living in it), but this is where Luke Skywalker trained as a Jedi!

Getting around

It really helps to be a Force user here. You can get around by leaping from bog to bog, and retrieve your ship when it inevitably sinks into the swamp. Luke's X-wing would have been lost forever without Yoda's Jedi powers!

Who's who on Dagobah

Yoda
After the Clone Wars, Yoda hid himself away on Dagobah, waiting for Luke or Leia to seek out his wisdom.

Luke Skywalker
A message from Obi-Wan Kenobi led Luke to Dagobah, where Yoda trained him in the ways of the Force.

R2-D2
Poor Artoo was almost eaten by a dragonsnake when he came to Dagobah with Luke!

BEWARE OF THE BOG!

HERE BE DRAGONSNAKES

So peaceful, it is. No jabber, just hut!

Typical weather

Thick fog and rainstorms.

LOTHAL

Lothal suffered badly under Imperial rule when it became a heavily polluted factory world. But since the planet was freed by daring rebels, it has recovered its former glory. Lush grasslands have regrown across most of the planet, while the one major city (simply called Capital City) is a gleaming hub of activity.

Typical weather

Fair, with striking cloud formations.

SEE LOTHAL'S STREET ART with SABINE WREN

Meet the famous Mandalorian rebel and artist on a walking tour of Capital City's Imperial-era graffiti. See Sabine's own rebel starbirds!

Nice planet—and nice color your speeder is!

LOOK OUT FOR LOTH-WOLVES!

Who's who in Lothal

Ezra Bridger
This young rebel was born on Lothal. He lived a tough life here before joining a rebel group called the Spectres.

Kanan Jarrus
Jedi Kanan trained Ezra in the ways of the Force. He sacrificed himself to save his fellow Spectres on Lothal.

Where to eat

Old Jho's Pit Stop

Its original owner, Jho, is sadly long gone. But you'll still find a tasty mug of spicebrew and slice of Jogan fruit cake. Don't forget to order a side of blue milk custard!

Speeder bike

LOTHAL GHOST TOURS

See this pretty planet from the sky on board the *Ghost*–the rebel ship that took on the Empire and won!

TOP 3 MUST SEES!

1. Grasslands and gorges

Explore Lothal's rolling countryside to find towering rock spires, "singing" spine trees, long-eared Loth-cats, and more!

2. Capital city

Forget its past as a polluted factory town. Lothal's capital now attracts visitors from across the galaxy.

3. Loth-wolves

Don't miss a chance to meet these mysterious creatures. They have a strong link to the Force and sometimes even speak!

Hera Syndulla

This Twi'lek rebel led the fight against the Empire on Lothal. She then joined the wider galactic rebellion.

Grand Admiral Thrawn

The Emperor sent this blue-skinned officer to Lothal with orders to crush the rebellion there.

Be more childlike on *Nevarro*

Find yourself on
Ahch-To

PLEASE
DON'T
EAT THE
PORGS

Ahch-To
Conservation
Society

LAZY SUMMER DAYS ON
KAMINO

CHAPTER FOUR

EVERYWHERE ELSE

You won't find these places on most galactic m
Some lie in the Unknown Regions beyond the
Outer Rim, while others are at coordinates no c
can quite agree on. Only the most seasoned
traveler should attempt these trips!

KAMINO

If you like swimming, you'll love this watery world. But don't expect to find any beaches—Kamino is all ocean, from no-coast to no-coast! The cities rise above the water on stilts, and if you want to keep dry, you'll need to stay inside them. It's always raining everywhere else!

What to pack

1. An umbrella
2. A towel
3. A snorkel

KAMINOANS:
WE STICK OUR NECK OUT FOR YOU!

YOU'RE NEVER ALONE WITH A CLONE

The perfect souvenir of a trip to Kamino!

Going outside in this weather, I am not!

GO BY AIR WHALE!

Typical weather

Heavy rain with occasional very heavy rain.

Jedi starfighter

72

TOP 3 MUST SEES!

1. Air whales

Also known as aiwhas, these majestic creatures can fly and swim—worth remembering if you take a ride on one!

2. Tipoca City

The high-tech capital of Kamino is made up of 12 enormous, elevated domes, linked by rain-soaked landing platforms.

3. Cloning facilities

The Kaminoans are famous for their cloning skills. For the right price, they'll happily make an exact copy of you!

Who's who on Kamino

Jango Fett
This bounty hunter agreed to live on Kamino so that its scientists could create an army of clones based on him!

Boba Fett
Jango's "son" is really a clone, created on Kamino. He grew up hating the Jedi, and became a bounty hunter like his "father."

Jango's clones
Millions of the troopers who fought in the Clone Wars were copies of Jango, grown in laboratories on Kamino.

Obi-Wan Kenobi
Few people knew that Kamino existed until Obi-Wan set out to find the planet!

★★★ Kamino reviews

Clone0000004
I really like it here. Not sure if my fellow clones would agree, though!
☆☆☆☆☆

Clone0000005
I really like it here. Not sure if my fellow clones would agree, though!
☆☆☆☆☆

AHCH-TO

This distant world is the ultimate galactic getaway. Almost no one knows where it is, and when Luke Skywalker learned of its location, he kept it a closely guarded secret! Long ago, it was home to the first Jedi Temple, but now its biggest attraction is millions of ultra-cute porgs!

 Typical weather
Cold, wet, and windy.

★★★ **Ahch-To** review

 FalconFlyer
Wwarrrrgwaaaahrroo!
☆☆☆☆☆

Temple Island

Who's who on Ahch-To

 **Luke Skywalker**
Luke spent years living alone here, when he believed the Jedi Order should come to an end.

 **Rey**
Rey pieced together a map to find Luke on Ahch-To, and convinced him to train her as a Jedi.

DOS AND DON'TS ON AHCH-TO

Do feed the porgs. The beakless birds enjoy fish-flavored treats!

Do visit the ancient Jedi village ruins on Temple Island.

Don't eat the porgs. Even if a Wookiee tells you they are delicious.

Don't damage the ruins—the birdlike Caretakers won't like it!

GO GREEN with a glass of THALA-SIREN MILK!

It's salty!

💼 What to pack

1. A map—this place is impossible to find without one!

2. Something to read—ideally one of the ancient Jedi texts.

3. Food and drink—unless you want to live off the green milk of the thala-siren!

Cute you may be. Judge me by my sighs you must not!

PORG PRESERVATION AREA

RESPECT OUR RUINS!

Keep to the paths on Temple Island

No fires or camping

Please keep use of the Force to a minimum

THANK YOU

— the Caretakers

R2-D2
Luke's old droid traveled to Ahch-To with Rey and reminded him of his old life as a rebel hero.

Porgs
These cuddly, cliff-dwelling birds get everywhere on Temple Island!

NEVARRO

This volcanic world was famous for the Mandalorians who made their home here after the Empire took control of their home planet. But now most of them are gone or have been forced to hide underground. The main draw for travelers to Nevarro is the chance to spot famous bounty hunters relaxing between their missions.

See the famous **LAVA FIELDS** on a **BOUNTY HUNTER TRANSPORT** tour.

It's Nevarro's **HOTTEST** *ticket!*

Traveler's tip

Bounty hunters accept payment to seek out any target. If you think a bounty hunter might be looking for you, don't make their job easier by going to Nevarro!

Just a tourist, I am!

Who's who on Nevarro

The Mandalorian
Din Djarin is a bounty hunter known as "the Mandalorian." He is part of a group of Mandalorians that live in the sewers.

The Child
The Mandalorian brought this young member of a familiar-looking species to Nevarro as his prisoner. But he decided to team up with him instead!

Hunt no further for fabulous souvenirs

at Nevarro City Bazaar

TOP 3 MUST SEES!

1. Nevarro City Common House

The Bounty Hunters Guild uses this eatery as an unofficial HQ. Lots of deals are done over dinner here!

2. Lava river cruise

Take a keelboat trip down the fiery rivers underneath Nevarro City. Watch out for the pesky lava meerkats, though!

3. Twi'lek healing baths

Imagine you are relaxing on the Twi'lek home planet of Ryloth with a spa treatment at this Nevarro hangout.

How much for the little green guy?

Typical weather

Hot and hazy.

CHILD FRIENDLY DESTINATION ✓

IG-11
This droid bounty hunter blew itself up on Nevarro in order to protect the Child.

Greef Karga
Mando's contact at the Bounty Hunters Guild can usually be found in the Common House eatery.

77

EXEGOL

There is one simple word of advice for anyone going to Exegol: don't! This Sith power base is an always gloomy, desert world, where the locals are all dedicated to the dark side. After the mighty Jedi Rey defeated Darth Sidious here, she got away as fast as she could!

What to pack

1. Nothing. Just don't come here!

2. Seriously, throw away your suitcases!

3. Sell your best starship and stay at home!

Greetings from **EXEGOL**

You'll wish you weren't here!

-SITH THRONE- NO SITTING!

Who's who on Exegol

Darth Sidious
The former Emperor hid himself away on Exegol for many years, plotting to bring the galaxy back

Snoke
The once supreme leader of the First Order was created in a laboratory here as a puppet for

Sith TIE fighter

CELEBRATE THE SITH

At the **1,000th EXEGOL EXPO!**
(Black TIE only)

TOP 3 MUST NOT SEES!

1. The Sith Citadel

The base of the mysterious Sith Eternal cult is a giant black box, floating just above the scarred surface of Exegol.

2. The Throne of the Sith

At the heart of the Sith Citadel is one of the galaxy's most powerful but least comfortable seats!

3. Star Destroyer scrapyards

When the Resistance won the Battle of Exegol, the Sith's new fleet of Star Destroyers crashed on the planet's surface.

Typical weather

Always stormy. Did we mention staying away?

Loved this place, Darth Vader would have!

Ben Solo
Kylo Ren became Ben Solo once more when he made sure Rey's story didn't end on Exegol.

Sith Troopers
Their armor may be on the bright side, but these Exegol-born brutes are all about the dark side!

79

GLOSSARY

POWER! UNLIMITED POWER!

Emperor
The ruler of the Empire.

asteroid
A large space rock.

bounty hunter
Someone who is paid to find or destroy people or objects.

carbonite
A strong metal used to preserve materials before they are transported across the galaxy.

civilization
A well-organized and developed area and group of people.

credits
Metal coins or chips used as money.

clone
An identical copy of a living thing, created in a lab.

Clone Wars
A series of galaxy-wide battles between a group of planets and their enemies. It led to the Empire ruling most of the galaxy.

dark side
The evil side of the Force that feeds off fear and hatred.

Death Star
A huge Imperial battle station, with enough firepower to destroy an entire planet.

droid
A robot that is programmed to work for a certain purpose or person.

Empire
A cruel government that ruled the galaxy under the leadership of Emperor Palpatine, a Sith Lord.

First Order
A powerful organization created from the remains of the Empire. Its aim was to take control of the galaxy.

The Force
The energy that flows through all living things. It can be used for good or evil.

galaxy
A group of millions of stars and planets.

hijack
To take control of something without permission.

hologram
A special image made from light of something that is not there.

hyperdrive
Part of a starship that allows it to travel faster than the speed of light.

Imperial
Something from or belonging to the Empire.

Imperial Army
The Empire's huge army.

Imperial era
The period when the Empire ruled the galaxy.

Jedi
People who can sense the energy created by all living things, and use it for good.

Jedi Order
An ancient group of Force users that promotes peace and justice throughout the galaxy.

lightsaber
A swordlike weapon with a blade of pure energy that is used by Jedi and Sith.

mudtrooper
A soldier of the Empire who has specialist training to fight on muddy planets.

podracer
A super-fast vehicle that flies close to the ground.

rebel
Someone who rises up to fight against the current ruler.

Rebel Alliance
The group that resisted and fought the Empire.

Resistance
The group that defended the galaxy from the First Order.

scavenger
Someone who searches through worthless junk to find useful things.

Sith
An ancient group of Force users who seek to use the dark side of the Force to gain power.

Sith Lord
A high-ranking member of the Sith.

smuggler
Someone who transports illegal goods.

spaceport
A place where starships and people can leave or arrive on a planet.

speeder
A powered flying vehicle.

stormtrooper
A soldier of the Empire and the First Order.

INDEX

Penguin
Random
House

Senior Editor Helen Murray
Project Art Editor Jenny Edwards
Designer James McKeag
Production Editor Siu Yin Chan
Senior Production Controller Lloyd Robertson
Managing Editor Paula Regan
Managing Art Editor Jo Connor
Publisher Julie Ferris
Art Director Lisa Lanzarini
Publishing Director Mark Searle

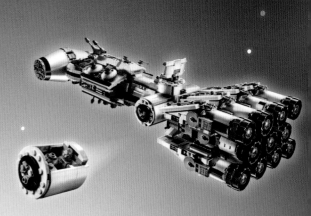

Book concept by Matt Jones.
DK would like to thank: Randi K. Sørensen, Heidi K. Jensen, Paul Hansford, and Martin Leighton Lindhardt at the LEGO Group; Jennifer Heddle, Michael Siglain, and Leland Chee at Lucasfim; Chelsea Alon at Disney Publishing; Guy Harvey for design assistance; Julia March for the index; Megan Douglass for proofreading.

Page design copyright ©2021 Dorling Kindersley Limited

First American Edition, 2021
Published in the United States by DK Publishing
1450 Broadway, Suite 801, New York, New York 10018

Page design copyright © 2021 Dorling Kindersley Limited

DK, a Division of Penguin Random House LLC
21 22 23 24 25 10 9 8 7 6 5
008–321718–April/2021

Published in Great Britain by Dorling Kindersley Limited.

A catalog record for this book is available from the Library of Congress.

ISBN 978-0-7440-2727-3 (trade edition)
978-0-7440-3005-1 (library edition)

DK books are available at special discounts when purchased in bulk for sales promotions, premiums, fund-raising, or educational use. For details, contact: DK Publishing Special
Markets, 1450 Broadway, Suite 801, New York, New York 10018
SpecialSales@dk.com

Printed and bound in China

For the curious

www.dk.com

www.LEGO.com/starwars

www.starwars.com